SPIRITUAL CHESS

Spiritual Warfare:

Bible Prophecy:

Dispensationalism

SPIRITUAL CHESS

Spiritual Warfare: Bible Prophecy: Dispensationalism

A Novel by Nathaniel Stone Jones

Editor: Nathaniel Stone Jones

Publisher: Stone Jones Publishing

SPIRITUAL CHESS

Spiritual Warfare: Bible Prophecy: Dispensationalism

Copyright © 2021 by Nathaniel Stone Jones

All Scriptures here are taken from the New King James Version of the Bible.

Cover Design and Photo Arrangements by Nathaniel Stone Jones

ISBN: 978-1-954425-99-6

DEDICATION

This book is dedicated to anyone and everyone who are willing to accept the free salvation offer of the Most-High God and have your name written into the Book of Life. That will enable you to receive a glorified body and make that magnificent journey throughout the universe during the Rapture of the Church. And so will we as God's children remain forever in the presence of the Lord.

For as many as are led by the Spirit of God, they are the sons of God. For you have not received the spirit of bondage again to fear; but you have received the Spirit of adoption, whereby we cry, Abba, Father. The Spirit itself bear witness with our spirit, that we are the children of God: And if children of God, and joint heirs with Christ; if so be that we suffer with *him*, that we may be also glorified together. For I reckon that the sufferings of this present time *are* not worthy *to be compared* with the glory which shall be revealed in us, *Romans 8: 14-18.*

And we know that all things work together for good to them that love God, to them who are called according to *His* purpose. For whom he did foreknow, he also did predestinate *to be* conformed to the image of his Son, that we might be the firstborn among many brothers, Romans 8:28-29.

ACKNOWLEDGMENTS

"We must stop confusing religion with spirituality. Religion is a set of rules, regulations and rituals created by humans, which were supposed to help people spiritually. Due to human imperfection, religion has become corrupt, political, divisive, and a tool for power struggle. Spirituality is not theology or ideology. It is simply a way of life, pure and original as given by the Most-High God. Spirituality is a network linking us to the Trinity, the universe, and to each other." Haile Selassie.

I want to give special thanks to the following authors, producers, etc. whose valuable contributions has enabled me to put together this novel "Spiritual Chess -Spiritual Warfare: Bible Prophecy: Dispensationalism."

A History of Chess: The Original 1913 Edition: H.J.R. Murray ... *https://www.amazon.com/History-Chess-Original-1913/dp/163220293X.*

The Truth About Angels: Authors Dr. John Bechtle and Dr. Paul Eymann, Christian Answers Network. P O Box 1167, Marysville, WA 98270 – 1167.

Satan, Demons, and the power of Darkness: All Rights Reserved for Diane Dew, P.O. Box 340945, Milwaukee, WI 53234.

2028 The End of The World https://www.youtube.com/watch?v=6AvxP5pRWsY. The movie is based on the book "Undeniable Biblical Proof." (Written by Gabriel Ansley Erb).

The Summary Chart on the Attributes of God - The Holy Trinity. As Defined by Charles H. Spurgeon.

Shutterstock Images https://www.shutterstock.com.

123RF Stock Images *https://www.**123rf**.com.*

And special considerations to Jude Iannelli for his graphic contributions, and to my nephew, author Antonne M. Jones, who inspired me to become a writer.

TABLE OF CONTENTS

ABOUT THE AUTHOR

Nathaniel Stone Jones is the author of both *"The Mandate of Stone Jones – Never Give Up,"* and *"Spiritual Chess- Books I and II."*

He was born and raised in Philadelphia, PA in the USA. In 1972, he graduated from Cheyney University in Pennsylvania with a Bachelor of Science Degree in Chemistry.

In 1973, he moved to Rochester, N.Y. to work as a chemist for Eastman Kodak Chemicals.

In 1975, he was fortunate to move to Oslo, Norway to live and to study, and he remained there for 11 years. After a spiritual encounter he had in Oslo that adversely affected his life, he returned to the USA in 1986.

Details of that encounter are described in his first book *"Never Give Up."* As a result of the encounter Nathaniel had in Oslo that led to his return to the U.S.A., he made a vow to learn more about the spiritual world. So, since 1990, he has been studying continuously regarding spiritual warfare and Bible prophecy.

And this novel is the culmination of what he has learned. And now, the author wants to share with you some of what he has learned about how the spiritual world operates.

The author also considers himself blessed to have followed several times the five-year Bible teachings of Dr. Vernon McGee and the "Thru the Bible Radio" program. That teaching contributed greatly to him gaining a comprehensive understanding of spiritual matters. It's important that we learn as much as possible for ourselves about such matters, rather than rely solely on any one person, minister, church, custom, religion, etc. Because eternity is a very long time if we should make the wrong choices. God's "word" is available for all to learn and understand.

INTRODUCTION

SPIRITUAL WARFARE: BIBLE PROPHECY: DISPENSATIONALISM

There is a method to the madness, and it's all about God preparing an eternal Kingdom for His children - that is those human beings who accept the Lord as their personal savior. They will spend eternity in heaven (New Jerusalem) in the presence of the Lord. Many are called but few are chosen, because it's not an easy task to overcome the wiles of the devil and his demons. They place many obstacles in our paths to prevent us from making peace with our Savior to become children of the Most-High God.

Spiritual warfare describes the type trials and tribulations we experience in life in the spiritual realm,
compared to those we encounter in the physical or secular realm, as represented by the board game called chess.

2 Peters 1: 20-21.
Bible prophecy is a divine revelation or message inspired by God. Prophets have delivered messages from God as they were moved by the Holy Spirit.

Consequently, no prophecy of Scripture is of any private interpretation,
for prophecy never came by the will of man, but by holy men of God.

Dispensationalism is the method of interpreting history according to how God divides his work and purposes towards mankind. There are seven major periods of time all total.

The Disclaimer

The author, Nathaniel Stone Jones, wrote this novel based on his personal spiritual encounters, his biblical learnings, and his beliefs, and he doesn't minimize the importance others place on their religion (Hinduism, Islam, Mormonism, Christian denominations, etc.), or whether one doesn't believe in God at all. His sole purpose here is to emphasize that the spiritual world is for real, and it can be a very dangerous place for humans to live in.

All scriptures quoted here are from the King James version of the Bible, and they conform to the teachings of the Christian religion. However, since the author have little working knowledge of other religions, he will elaborate solely on how the spiritual world works according to the Bible.

CHAPTER 1

CHESS VS SPIRITUAL CHESS

Spiritual chess or "spiritual warfare" is a term used by the author to bring into focus the effects the spiritual world has on our lives, whether directly or indirectly. It describes the experiences we have on the battlefields of life in the spiritual realm, as compared to those we have in the physical or secular realm. Whereas the chess board game depicts humans battling humans using weapons and the latest technology available at the time, spiritual chess incorporates those same elements plus the trials and tribulations we encounter when influenced by spiritual forces. Most people fail to realize that all human beings are born into a world of unending battles on both the secular and spiritual levels, and the overall success that an individual may experience during their lifespan depends on the relationship they have with God, the Creator of all things.

The board game of chess is synonymous with warfare on the secular level, and it's one of the oldest continuous games ever invented. It has been played throughout the ages by men, women, and children of all walks of life. The game is the representation of two enemy forces making attempts to defeat each other on the battlefield. While chess has been in existence since the mid-7th century, it's remarkable that the same strategies, objectives, and fundamentals are still being used in the game today. Except for the powerful and quickly developing double push of the pawn, the bishop's long-range attack angle, and the addition of the powerful queen, the chess pieces has basically remained the same since the game's inception.

The name for chess originated from the word chaturanga, meaning the four divisions of the military based on that period, i.e., the infantry (foot soldiers), cavalry (on horseback), elephantry (the elephant brigade), and chariotry (motorized vehicle soldiers), which are represented in modern chess by the pawn, the knight, the bishop, and the rook pieces respectively. Unverified sources place the origin of chess as far back as 100 A.D., and the earliest verifiable sources place the precursor to the game to the Gupta Empire in the 6th Century in Northern India near where Afghanistan is situated today. The Muslims conquered Persia in the mid-7th century, and chess was carried back to the Muslim world into North Africa, and later into Europe. In ancient Islam, the game was known as shatranj, and referred to the "Shah" as the lead piece. Once the game reached Europe, the Shah was replaced with the "king" as the most important piece.

Like in all forms of warfare, battles may have different ways to lead to victory or defeat. In chess, the variations between the moves on the chessboard can be as vast as there are grains of sand on this earth. Basically, there are three main parts to the game (the opening, the mid-game, and the endgame). It helps to have a strong opening game, but a player must maintain a good mid and endgame too to ensure victory. Therefore, every move one makes is important, because they can put you in a weaker or stronger position for the rest of the game.

The overall strategy of chess is to trap or checkmate your opponent's king through a series of attacks combined with a good defense. The moves should be coordinated (teamwork) to render the king vulnerable by capturing or taking enemy pieces by means of **forks** (attacking two pieces at one time which is protecting another piece more powerful than itself), **skewers** (forcing a more powerful piece to move so a less powerful piece can be captured), and pins (attacking a certain piece which is protecting another piece more powerful than itself).

Spiritual chess or spiritual warfare began in heaven long before the board game was even conceived of. It started when Satan, a cherub angel and God's most treasured creation, revolted against God when he tempted Adam and Eve to sin in the Garden of Eden.

And it continues today. In Revelation 12:7-9, it's indicated that war is being fought in heaven between God's faithful angels and Lucifer, the dragon, and his demons. Satan's forces are defeated, and they are hurled down to earth. Woe to the inhabitants of earth, for Satan's eviction from heaven leads to what is described as the beginning of the Great Tribulation era on earth – seven years of the worst conditions to ever face mankind.

In spiritual warfare, the major players are not pawns, bishops, knights, queens, or kings. They are the Trinity, the Father, the Son, and the Holy Spirit, and their faithful angels on one side. While Lucifer or Satan and his fallen angels or demons are on the other side. And then, there is mankind caught in between.

In regular chess, on the spiritual level the king is the most central character on the battlefield. In spiritual chess, it is the **individual** person that is the most central character on the battlefield.

Whether they go down in defeat or not is determined by which side they are on when thier final breath is taken. Will they be in the presence of the creator for eternity, or not? That is the ultimate question for everyone to answer to.

Characters on the Chessboard

The White side of the board

1g The King or Jehovah,

1e The Rook or the Holy Spirit,

1c The Rook or the Holy Spirit

2h A Human,

2g A Human,

2f A Human,

2b A Human

3d The Bishop or the Seraph,

3c A Human

4e The Queen Position (Christ),

4a A Human,

5d A Human

6h The Bishop or the Cherub

The Black side of the board

8g The King or Lucifer,

8d The Rook or the Grim Reaper,

8b The Knight or the Horned-Demon,

8a The Rook or the Grim Reaper

7h A Human,

7f A Human,

7c The Queen,

7b A Human

6g A Human,

6F The Bishop or the Dragon,

6d A Human, 6a A Human

5f The Bishop or the Dragon

CHAPTER 2

THE HOLY TRINITY

In the spirit world there is a hierarchy difference for all participants of spiritual warfare.

At the top of the spiritual hierarchy is the **Trinity**, who is represented by **Jehovah** (the Father), **Jesus** (the Son), and the **Holy Ghost** (the Comforter.)

The Triune God are all-powerful, have prior knowledge and awareness of all things, and they are present everywhere.

They are divine, have benevolence toward human beings, and they have a disposition for forgiving.

They uphold what is right or lawful, and they are fair in treatment or punishment.

Yet, they possess a divine wrath or retribution for sin.

The Father

is the "mind or head" of
the Trinity. He is known by
the following names,
which helps to describe His
character.

1. Jehovah Elohim
The eternal creator
(Genesis 2:4-5)

2. Jehovah Adonai –
The Lord our sovereign;
Master Jehovah
(Genesis 15:2, 8)

3. Jehovah Jireh –
The Lord will see or provide
(Genesis 22:8-14)

4. Jehovah Nissi
The Lord our banner
(Exodus 17:15)

5. Jehovah Rapha
The Lord our healer
(Exodus 15:26)

6. Jehovah-shalom
   The Lord our peace
   (Judges 6:24)

7. El Shaddai
   The Almighty Powerful
   One.

8. Jehovah - M'Kaddesh
   The Lord who sacrifices

9. Yahweh
   The Self Existent
   Eternal God

10. El Elyon
   The Most High God

No one comes to the Father except through **Christ** who is the "body" of God.

John 1:1-3
In the beginning was the Word, and the Word was with God, and the Word was God.
Through Him all things were made; without Him nothing was made that has been made.
The "Word" is another name for our Savior.

John 3:16
For God so loved the world that He gave His only begotten Son, that whosoever believe in Him shall not perish but have eternal life.

1 John 3:8
Christ was crucified for the forgiveness of sins for all mankind (i.e., past, present, and future.)

He was manifested that He might destroy the works of the devil.

John 14:26
But the Comforter whom the Father will send in my name (Jesus), will teach you all things,
and bring all things to your remembrance,
whatsoever I have said unto you.

1 John 4:4 and 1 Corinthian 3:16
Do you know that you are the "temple" of God, and that the "Spirit" of God dwells within you? Greater is He that is in you than he that is in the world.

It is the **Holy Spirit** that converts us into becoming "born-again" believers.

CHAPTER 3

GOD'S FAITHFUL ANGELS

The next level in the spiritual warfare hierarchy are the angels.

Hebrews 1:14
The word "angel" is derived from the Greek for "messenger,"
but God's messengers also include ordinary people, prophets,
priests, church leaders and more.

Hebrews 12:22
Angels were all created at the same time.
While Scripture gives no definite figures, we know that the number of
angels is very great.

There are nine different types of angels that are loyal to God,
and they are divided into three different classes (or Spheres.)

FIRST SPHERE OR CHOIR:
ANGELS WHO ARE CLOSEST TO GOD'S THRONE

Isaiah 6:2

SERAPH
(SERAPHIM)

These are the most
powerful angels in
God's kingdom.
Their primary duty is to
praise Him and to pro-
tect His throne.

They have six wings
each - two to cover their
face, two to cover their
feet, and two to fly.

CHERUB
(CHERUBIM)

These fierce angels are the second highest in God's hierarchy, and they have apocalypse power.

They protect God's throne, and they intercede in affairs on earth.

Cherubs each have four wings and four faces - one of a cherub, a man, an eagle, and a lion.

Colossians 1:16

THRONES

These are the angels who dispense God's divine judgments, and they carry out His decisions.

Lower hierarchy angels must seek their permission to gain access to God.

Thrones bodies are covered with eyes all over, and they are represented as fiery wheels.

MANAGEMENT LEVEL ANGELS

DOMINIONS

These are the angels that lead and regulate the duties of other angels.
They also give power to government and authoritative figures on earth.

They have the appearance of humans with wings.

VIRTUES

These angels, "the shining ones," are known for their unyielding courage, and for having control of nature, and motion.

They perform miracles and encourage humans to strengthen their faith in God.

Colossians 1:16

POWERS

These warrior angels control the border between heaven and earth.
They have power over the devil, and they fight evil everywhere.

They help people cast out vices and evil,
and they are associated with the birth and death of humans.

ANGELS THAT DEAL DIRECTLY IN THE AFFAIRS OF HUMANS

Colossians 1:16

PRINCIPALITIES

These angels are associated with governing over nations, cities, and municipalities.

This includes matters related to religion, politics, economics, etc.

They lead all the angels on earth, and they guard against the invasion of evil angels.

GUARDIAN ANGELS

These angels act as our personal guardians.

They deliver our prayers to God and His messages to us.

Their duties include nurturing, counseling, and healing human beings.

ARCHANGELS

The prefix 'arch' means ruling or chief in Greek, and it usually refer to an archangel. There are seven archangels varying from faith to faith. Scriptures tell of the archangels' great abilities as healers and guides, intervening with assistance in many of life's challenging situations.

They are sent by God to deliver important messages to mankind, and they empower humans to develop a stronger faith.They travel throughout the universe fighting evil

Archangel Michael, whose name means [he who is as God], is the leader of all the angels. He is the angel of protection, and a patron of righteousness, mercy, and justice. He is often depicted as a warrior carrying a sword. He helps to release fear and doubt and supports us in making life changes.

Archangel Raphael, whose name means 'God heals', is the archangel dealing with physical and emotional healing, and he help reduce our addictions and cravings. He aids us in restoring and maintaining harmony and peace.

Archangel Gabriel's name means "God is my strength";. She is often portrayed holding a trumpet. As the patron of communications, she acts as a messenger of God. She helps writers, teachers, journalists, and artists to convey their message, and she assists in all areas related to children, including conception, pregnancy, childbirth, and child rearing.

Archangel Jophiel's name means "beauty of God". She helps us to see and maintain beauty in life and supports us in thinking beautiful thoughts and in staying positive. She watches over artists supporting in creating beautiful art and heals negativity and chaos. She is also the patron saint of animals and the environment,

Archangel Ariel, whose name means "lion or lioness of God". Her role is to protect the earth, its natural resources, ecosystems, and she assists in healing injured animals and all wildlife. It is believed that she also oversees the order of the physical universe and earth's natural resources.

Archangel Azrael's name means "whom God helps". He is often referred to as the "Angel of Death". He helps humans transition to death, and he helps loved ones on the earth in dealing with their grief and processing the loss. He also assists with transitions related to relationships, career, addictions, etc., helping us to navigate as smoothly as possible through life's changes.

Archangel Chamuel's name means "he who sees God". His mission is to bring peace to the world. He is believed to have all knowing vision seeing the interconnectedness between all things. He assists us in finding the strength and courage to face adversity, He also assist us in finding important aspects of our lives such as life purpose, a love relationship, a new job, and sup-portive friendships. He also helps us find solutions to problems.

Archangel Metatron supervises angels in heaven.

Metatron also leads the other angels in constantly praising God through music and chanting.

They record everything anyone in history has ever thought, said, written, or done.

ANGELS

Angels are supernatural
beings; and they are
not bound by the
laws of nature.

They do not have
physical bodies,
but they can appear
as humans on
occasion.

They are stronger
than man,
but not omnipotent
or all powerful.

They are more
knowledgeable than man,
but not omniscient or
all-knowing.

CHAPTER 4

FALLEN ANGELS

Fallen Angels are those angels who rebelled against God.

Ezekiel 28:14-15

LUCIFER

(otherwise known as the devil), was initially created as an anointed cherub.

He rebelled against God, along with one third of the angels.

The remaining 2/3 of the angels are faithful to God.

Lucifer has 4 heads and 4 wings, and is known for being a dragon, a serpent, and a lion.

John 10:10

Lucifer's motives are destructive, and they are designed to hinder the work of God, to deceive the nations, and to afflict mankind (physically, mentally, and spiritually).

1 Peter 5:8

Your adversary, the devil, is a roaring lion walking to and fro seeking whom he may conquer.

Ephesians 6:12
For we wrestle not against flesh and blood, but against principalities, (demons with supervision over nations), against powers (demons that possess human beings),

against the rulers of the darkness of this world (demons that manage Satan's worldly business),

against spiritual wickedness in high places (demons that oversee Satan's false religions).

Fallen angels
are subject to the rules of the Holy Trinity, and they testify to the divinity of the Messiah.

They recognize which humans are saved, and they are subject to them as well.

Matthew 12:43-45
Fallen angels can enter and leave a human's body at will, except for born-again believers who are baptized by the Holy Spirit.

Romans 16:20;
Revelation 20:1-3
Once God has used wicked angels to accomplish His purposes,

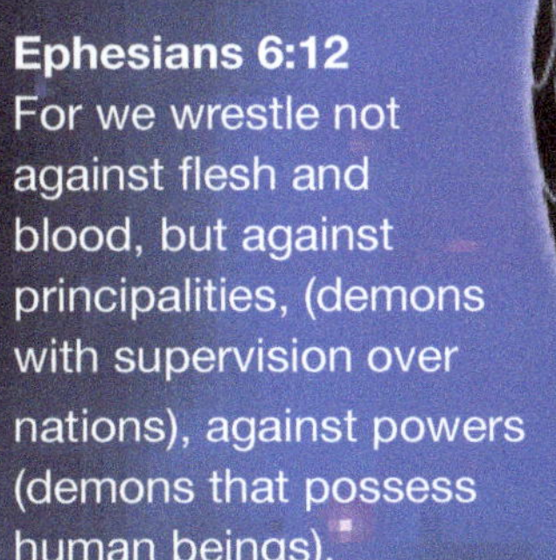

CHAPTER 5
HUMAN BEINGS

Human beings comprise the last level of the Spiritual Chess hierarchy.

Both faithful and fallen angels fight for the soul of every person born into this world.

Genesis 5:1-2
God created mankind in His image with a mind, a body, and a soul or spirit.

Most people consider a newborn child to be a gift from God.

Genesis 1:28
"Be fruitful and multiply; fill the earth and subdue it…"

However, we are born into a world of never-ending battles on both the secular and the spiritual levels.

But the overall success we will have in life depends on the relationship we have with our Creator.

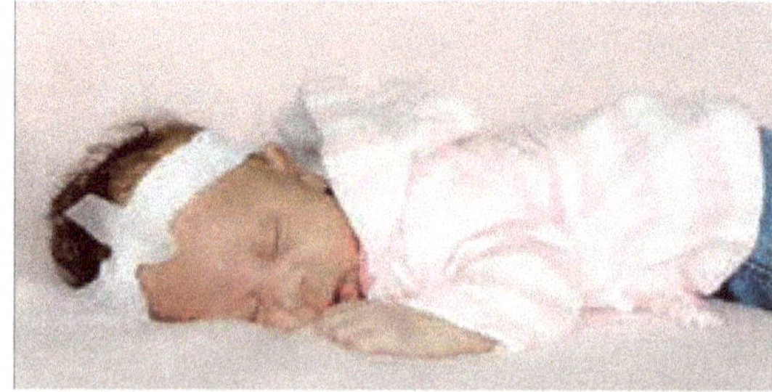

As spiritual beings, our souls are not subject to death or any form of extinction.

Therefore, we should be greatly concerned for where we will spend our eternity.

God is using humans on earth "to establish His eternal kingdom in heaven."

God gave man the ability to choose between good and evil, but He prohibited mankind from initiating contact with the spirit world.

Deuteronomy 18:10-14
Let no one be found among you... who practices divination or sorcery, interprets omens, engages in witchcraft, or casts spells, or who is a medium or spiritist who consults the dead.

Anyone who does these things is detestable to the Lord.

God does send angels to us in response to our prayers, but they normally do not make direct visible contact with man.

Ephesians 6:11
Therefore, put on the whole armor of God that you may be able to stand against the wiles of the devil.

CHAPTER 6

DISPENSATIONALISM

Dispensationalism is described as
God's work and purpose for mankind.

THE FIRST PERIOD IS THE

DISPENSATION OF INNOCENCE,

which lasted from
6000 B.C. to 4004 B.C.

Gen 1: 26-28; Gen 2: 15-17
God's commandment to Adam and Eve in the Garden of
Eden was to replenish the earth with children,
subdue the earth and take care of the garden.

They were to have dominion over the animals and abstain
from eating the fruit from the tree of knowledge of good
and evil.

Gen 3: 1-6; Gen 3: 17-19
The devil convinced them to eat the forbidden fruit anyway,
and that led to them being evicted from the Garden of Eden.

DISPENSATION OF CONSCIENCE

which lasted from

4004 B.C. to 2350 B.C.

Genesis 3:8 – 8:22
Adam and Eve inherited a sin nature,
and as punishment they had to learn how to produce their
own food to survive.

Mankind also became cursed by the changes affecting
womanhood and childbearing.

God promised that He would send Christ to bruise Satan for
leading mankind to sin.

Christ would be our Savior and redeem mankind for their
original sin.

The period ended with the coming of Noah and the flood.

DISPENSATION OF HUMAN GOVERNMENT

which lasted from

2350 B.C. TO 2000 B.C.

Genesis 9:1-3
God had destroyed life on earth with the flood,
and He arranged for Noah and his family to replenish mankind.

He promised Noah that He would never curse the earth again
with a worldwide flood, and He used the rainbow as a sign to fulfill
His promise.

He arranged for mankind to have dominion over the animal
kingdom, and He allowed for them to add eating meat to their diet.

The law of capital punishment was established then,
and it became acceptable to execute someone
for taking another person's life.

Genesis 11:7-9
About 325 years after the flood, the earth's inhabitants
began building the Tower of Babel as a great monument
to their solidarity and pride.

But God brought that construction to a halt, and that led to
the formation of different languages, cultures, nations, and human
governments.

THE FOURTH PERIOD IS THE

DISPENSATION OF PROMISE

which lasted from

2000 B.C. TO 1500 B.C.

Genesis 12:1-3

It started with the covenant that God made with Abraham to make him the father of a great nation,

and it continued through the lives of the patriarchs (Abraham, Isaac, and Jacob).

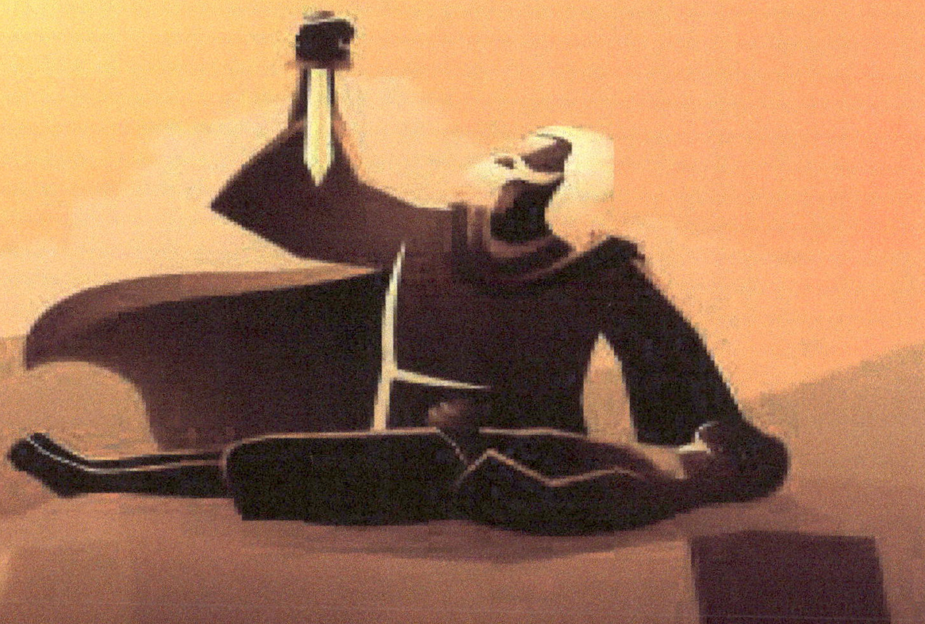

Exodus 12: 1-3

The period ended with the Exodus of the Jewish people from Egypt due to Abraham descendants' failure to obey God,

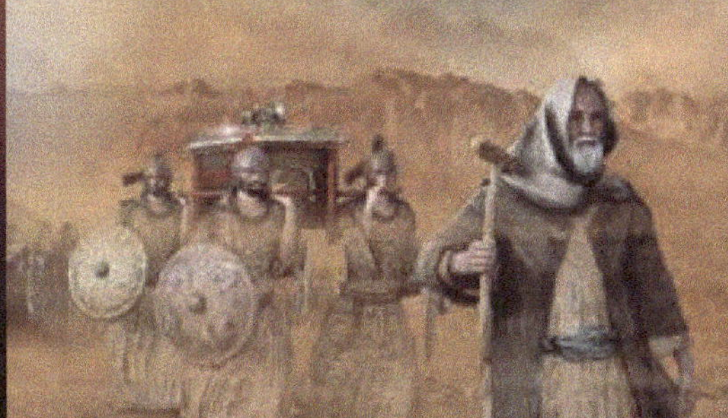

DISPENSATION OF LAW

which lasted from

1500 B.C. TO CHRIST'S DEATH

DISPENSATION OF GRACE OR THE CHURCH AGE.

This is the age in which we now live, and it is prophesized to last 2000 years following Christ's death.

4 B.C. to 6 B.C. - Christ was born during the reign of King Herod.

24 A.D. to 26 A.D. - Christ began his ministry at age 30.

27 A.D. to 29 A.D. – Christ's Ministry lasted 3 years. He was tried, executed, buried, and raised on the third day.

2027 A.D. to 2029 A.D. - The Grace Age ends, and the New Millennium begins.

THE RAPTURE OF THE CHURCH

2020 A.D. to 2022 A.D. - Although no one knows for sure when the Rapture will occur, it is prophesized to happen 7 years before the Great Tribulation end. All Born-again believers are predestined to go to heaven with Christ when He returns before the Great Tribulation takes place.

CHAPTER 7

Bible Prophecies and the Rapture of the Church

Throughout the Old and New Testaments over 2,500 prophecies have been predicted.

Over 2,000 of them are fulfilled and the remaining ones are being realized as we speak.

It is prophesied that God is preparing an eternal kingdom for His believers. Nothing can be more rewarding than becoming a child of the Most-High God.

We will become supernaturally much stronger physically, and much greater in knowledge.

Our growth potentials will be unlimited, and we will be able to freely roam the universe.

Everyone who make that journey to heaven must become transformed and made holy in the presence of God.

And all that is required to qualify to become a child of God is to accept the Lord as your personal savior.

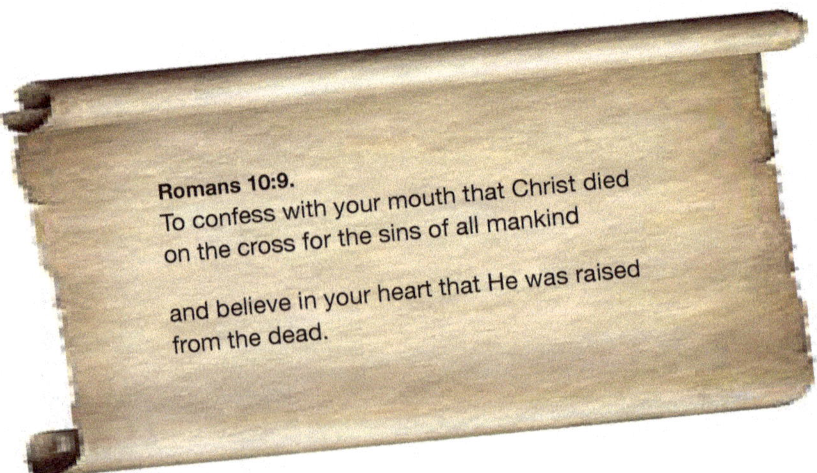

However, there is a deadline for accepting the Lord's free offer
of salvation.

For anyone who is fortunate to qualify for that magnificent
journey through space,
their earthly body will have to
be transformed.

1 Corinthians 15:51-54
*"Listen, I tell you a
mystery: We will not all
sleep, but we will all be
changed.*

*In an instant, in the
twinkling of an eye,
at the last trumpet shall
sound,*

*and the dead shall be
raised incorruptible,
and we shall all
be changed.*

*For this corruptible must
put on incorruption,
and this mortal must put
on immortality.*

*So, when this corruptible
shall have put on
incorruption,
and this mortal shall
have put on immortality,*

*then shall be brought to
pass the saying that is
written:*

*"Death is swallowed up
in victory,"*

1 Thessalonians 4:16-18

And, the Lord shall send His angels with a great sound of a trumpet,

and they shall gather his elect from the four winds,

from one end of heaven to the other,"

For, the Lord himself shall descend from heaven with a shout, with the voice of the archangel,

and with the trump of God: and the dead in Christ shall rise first:
then we which are alive and remain shall be caught
up together with them in the clouds,

to meet with the Lord in the air:

Omni
is the representation
of every believer,
from every country,

who have accepted
Christ as their
personal savior
during the 2000 years,
of the Grace Age.

and so, shall we forever be with the Lord.

Wherefore comfort one another with these words.

The Lord and His angels will lead God's children to the outer limits of the universe to heaven.

CHAPTER 8

THE GREAT TRIBULATION

Meanwhile, after the Lord has led His saints safely away from earth via the Rapture, and then the Great Tribulation will begin.

For the next seven years, the Lord will pour out His wrath upon those who rejected His free offer of salvation.

Matthews 24:29-30
"Immediately, after the tribulation of those days shall the sun be darkened,

and the moon shall not give her light,

and the stars shall fall from heaven, and the powers of the heavens shall be shaken:

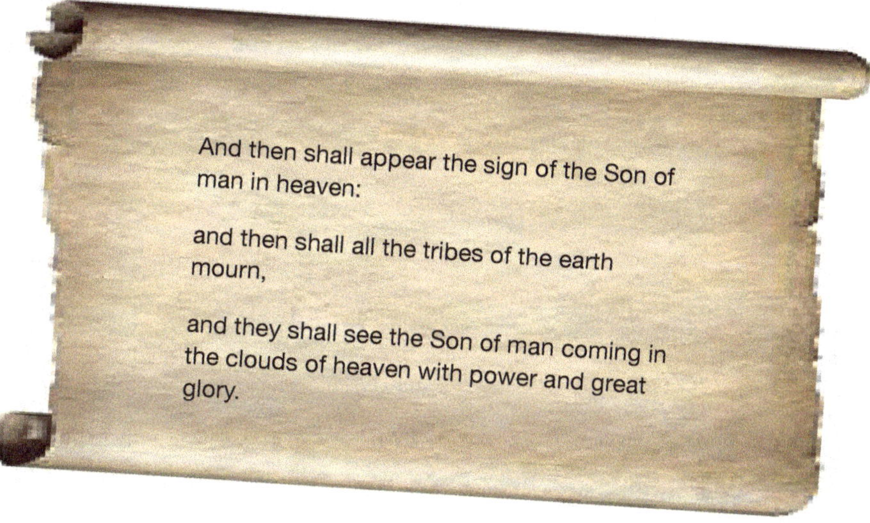

And then shall appear the sign of the Son of man in heaven:

and then shall all the tribes of the earth mourn,

and they shall see the Son of man coming in the clouds of heaven with power and great glory.

As a result of the Rapture, collisions will occur all over when people go missing while flying airplanes,

and while driving cars, buses, and trains.

Explosions will occur when workers disappear at manufacturing plants, power stations, chemical plants, military facilities, etc.

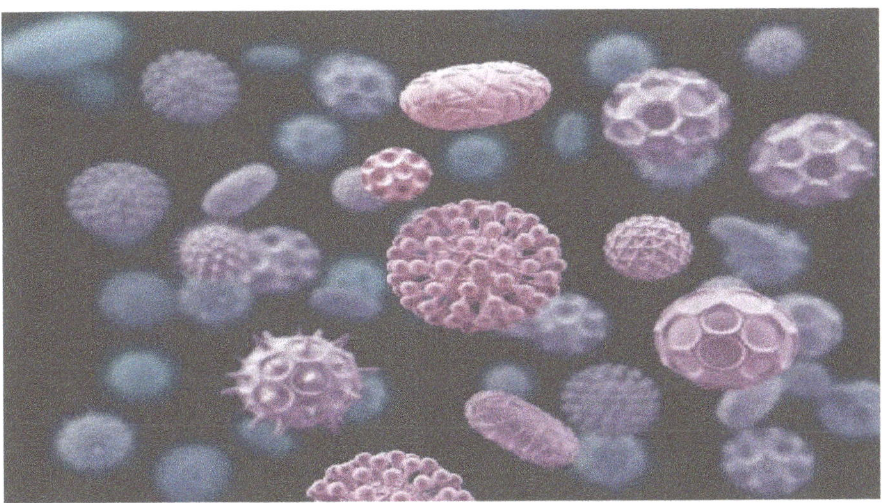

Countless lives will also be lost due to plagues and pestilences.

Natural disasters will occur worldwide, such as

monstrous wildfires,

floods,   tsunamis,

earthquakes,   droughts,

 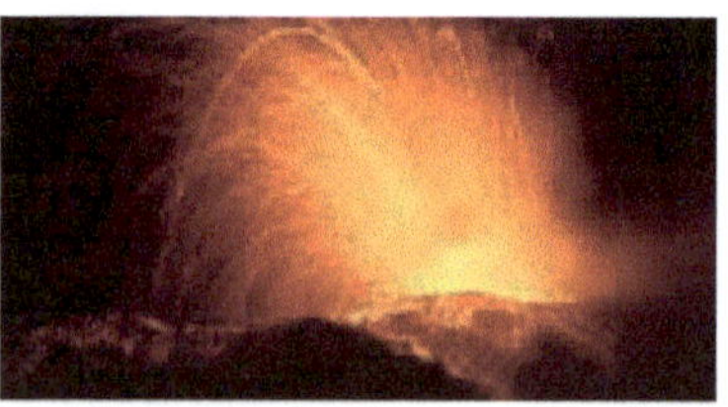

hurricanes and tornadoes.   volcanic eruptions.

Many lives will also be lost due to wars
being fought everywhere.

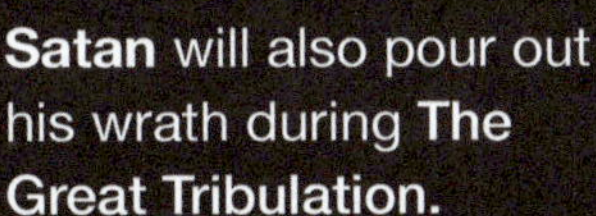

Satan will also pour out his wrath during **The Great Tribulation.**

He will establish a One World Government and appoint the **Anti-Christ** as his Supreme Leader.

They will gain total control over all transportation networks worldwide (trains, boats, airports).

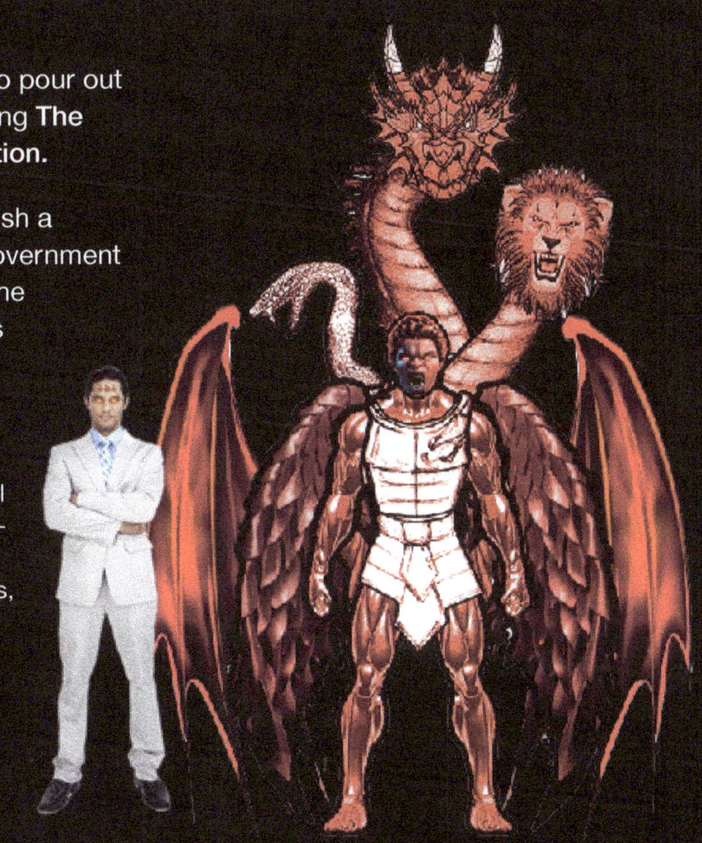

The whole planet will virtually become a prison planet, and Satan's goal will be to destroy anyone left behind.

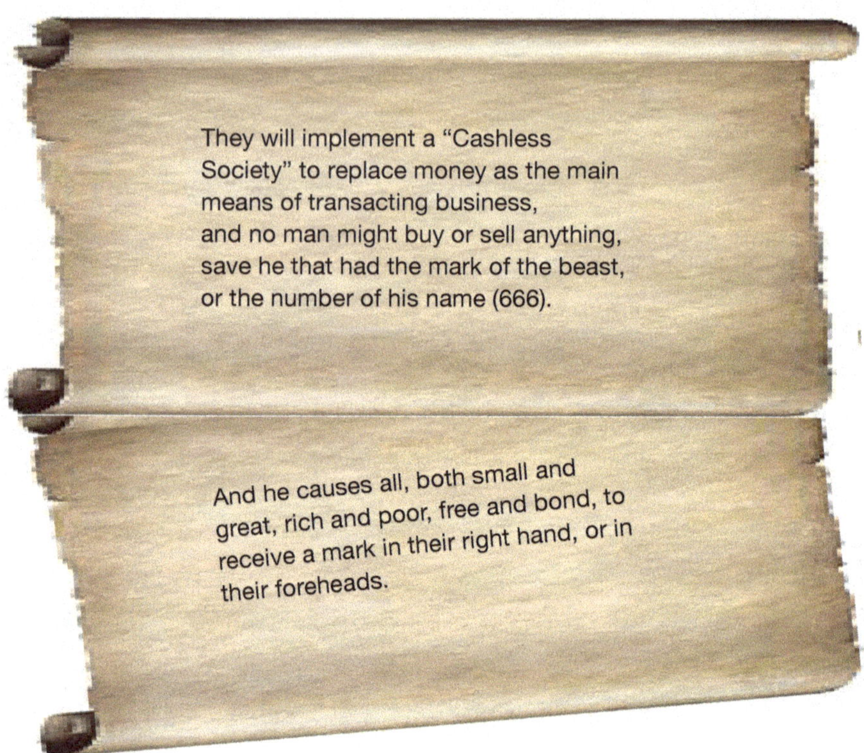

They will implement a "Cashless Society" to replace money as the main means of transacting business, and no man might buy or sell anything, save he that had the mark of the beast, or the number of his name (666).

And he causes all, both small and great, rich and poor, free and bond, to receive a mark in their right hand, or in their foreheads.

Anyone refusing to pledge allegiance to the Antichrist will be imprisoned, and they will be beheaded at the guillotine.

If anyone should accept the devil's mark they will be separated from the Most-High God forever.

After 3 ½ years into the Great Tribulation, the Battle of Armageddon is prophesized to take place.

That is when forces loyal to the Antichrist will gather in the mountains of Israel for a massive assault on the country.

The Lord will intervene and unleash supernatural forces to defeat Satan, the Antichrist, and the invading armies.

When a full seven years has past, the Great Tribulation will end.

The world will be destroyed and all life on earth will cease.

Satan will be bound, and the final judgment will begin.

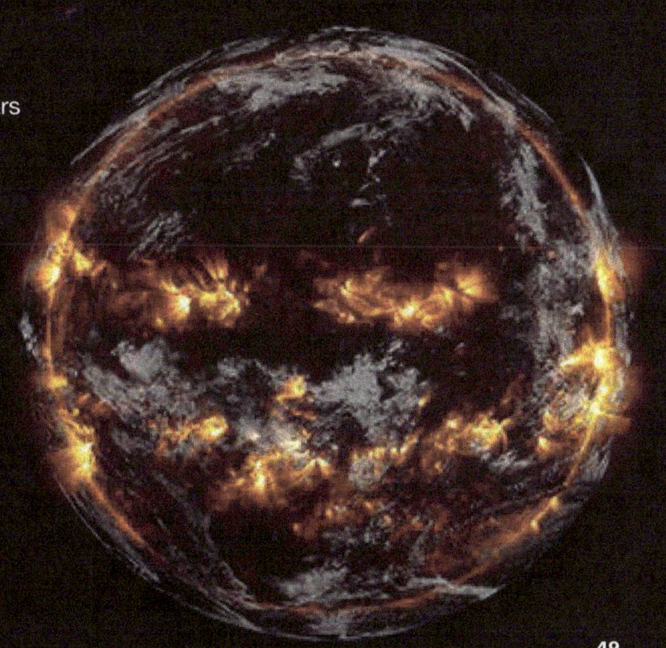

CHAPTER 9

NEW CREATION
NEW EARTH
NEW JERUSALEM
NEW HEAVEN

Then, the Seventh Dispensation called the Millennial Kingdom will begin.

God will replace the former earth with a New Earth.

Christ will rule over the planet for the next 1,000 years.

On the New Earth, only Born-Again saints will be allowed to enter the Kingdom.

That includes the resurrected Old Testament saints, and those saints who accepted God's salvation during the Great Tribulation.

In the book of Revelation
Chapters 21 and 22,
the Apostle John describes
how he saw a new heaven
and a new earth for the first heaven and
the first earth had passed away: and
there was no more sea.

He saw the Holy
City, New Jerusalem,
coming down out
of heaven,

prepared as a bride
beautifully dressed for her
husband.

"Look! God's dwelling
place is now among
the people,and He will
dwell with them.

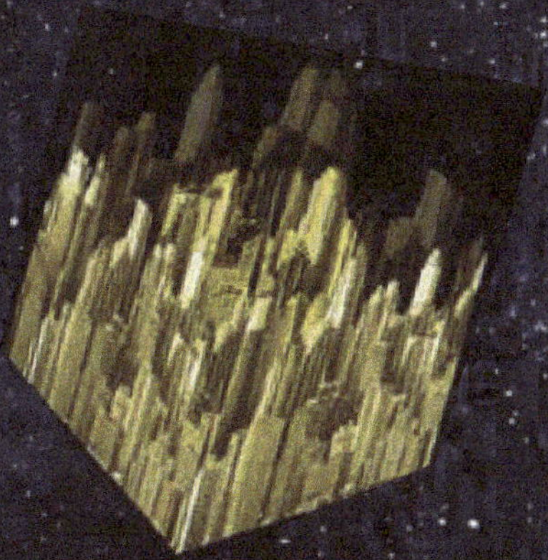

God created New
Jerusalem as the eternal
residence for those who
were raptured from the
grace age.

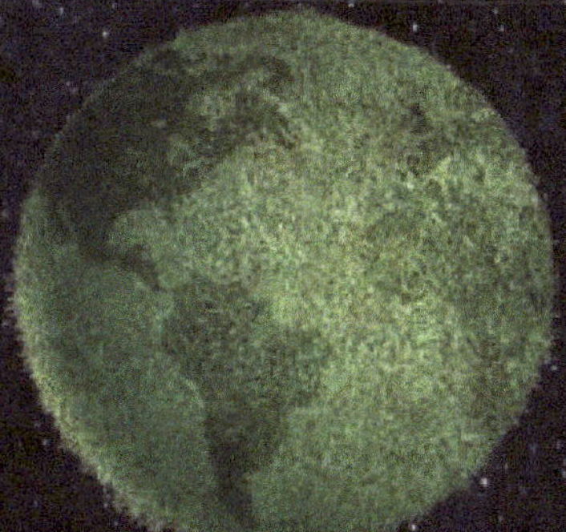

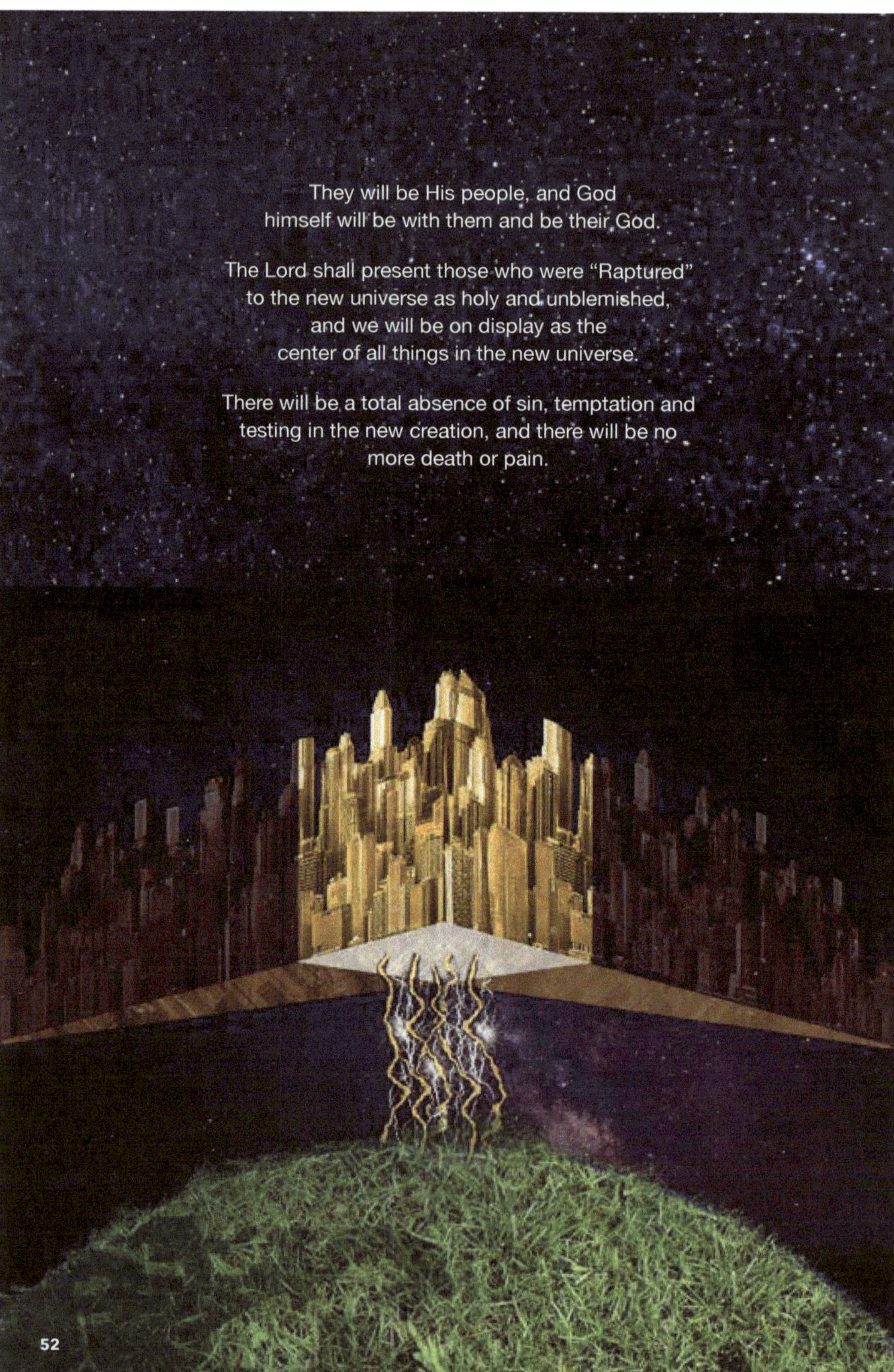
They will be His people, and God
himself will be with them and be their God.

The Lord shall present those who were "Raptured"
to the new universe as holy and unblemished,
and we will be on display as the
center of all things in the new universe.

There will be a total absence of sin, temptation and
testing in the new creation, and there will be no
more death or pain.

All things will be made new.

Matthew 19:29
And everyone that has forsaken
houses, or brethren, or sisters, or father, or mother,
or wife, or children, or lands, for my name's sake,
shall receive one hundredfold.

THE END

PHOTO/ILLUSTRATION CREDITS

PAGE 14:
JESUS IMAGE BY DENDIZ ©SHUTTERSTOCK.COM
HOLY FATHER IMAGE BY DUDA VASILII ©SHUTTERSTOCK.COM
HOLY SPIRIT IMAGE BY MIKE H ©SHUTTERSTOCK.COM

PAGE 18:
ANGEL WINGS IMAGE BY MR. SUTTIPON YAKHAM ©SHUTTERSTOCK.COM

PAGE 19:
ANGEL WINGS IMAGE BY MR. SUTTIPON YAKHAM ©SHUTTERSTOCK.COM
LION IMAGE BY ALEKSEYMARTYNOV ©123RF.COM
CHERUB IMAGE BY SEAMARTINI ©123RF.COM
EAGLE IMAGE BY REFLUO ©SHUTTERSTOCK.COM
THRONES ILLUSTRATION BY JUDE IANNELLI

PAGE 20:
ANGEL WINGS IMAGE BY MR. SUTTIPON YAKHAM ©SHUTTERSTOCK.COM
ARMOR IMAGE BY PIO3 ©SHUTTERSTOCK.COM
FIRE WOMAN BY MIKHAIL BAKUNOVICH ©SHUTTERSTOCK.COM
POWERS BY JIM LARKIN ©SHUTTERSTOCK.COM

PAGE 21:
PRINCIPALITIES IMAGE BY SATORI.ARTWORK ©SHUTTERSTOCK.COM
GUARDIAN ANGEL IMAGE BY ENNONA GAVRILOVA_ELLINA ©SHUTTERSTOCK.COM
GUARDIAN ANGEL WINGS IMAGE BY MARSHOT ©SHUTTERSTOCK.COM

PAGE 22:
MICHAEL IMAGE BY ATDIGIT ©SHUTTERSTOCK.COM
RAPHAEL IMAGE BY JULIA RAKETIC ©SHUTTERSTOCK.COM

PAGE 23:
GABRIEL IMAGE BY NNNMMM ©SHUTTERSTOCK.COM
JOPHIEL IMAGE BY NNNMMM ©SHUTTERSTOCK.COM
ARIEL IMAGE BY BABIN ©SHUTTERSTOCK.COM

PAGE 24:
AZREAL IMAGE BY NNNMMM ©SHUTTERSTOCK.COM
CHAMUEL IMAGE BY LANAN ©SHUTTERSTOCK.COM
METATRON IMAGE BY VARKA ©123RF.COM

PAGE 25:
ANGEL IMAGES BY
1A.ANGEL WINGS IMAGE BY MARSHOT ©SHUTTERSTOCK.COM
1B. ARMOR IMAGE BY PIO3 ©SHUTTERSTOCK.COM

2. WARPAINT©SHUTTERSTOCK.COM

3. BASHEERA DESIGNS ©SHUTTERSTOCK.COM

4. ANASTASIAROMB ©SHUTTERSTOCK.COM

PAGE 26:

LIONS HEAD IMAGE BY ALEKSEYMARTYNOV ©123RF.COM

DRAGONS HEAD IMAGE BY ULYANKIN ©123RF.COM

DRAGON WINGS IMAGE BY CHRISTOS GEORGHIOU ©SHUTTERSTOCK.COM

PAGE 27:

REAPER IMAGE BY DUDA VASILII ©SHUTTERSTOCK.COM

REAPER WINGS IMAGE BY MARSHOT ©SHUTTERSTOCK.COM

DRAGON IMAGE BY RALF JUERGEN KRAFT ©SHUTTERSTOCK.COM

DRAGON WINGS IMAGE BY CHRISTOS GEORGHIOU ©SHUTTERSTOCK.COM

REAPER WITH SICKLE IMAGE BY ROMARIOIEN ©SHUTTERSTOCK.COM

REAPER WINGS IMAGE BY MARSHOT ©SHUTTERSTOCK.COM

FEMALE ANGEL BY SHULDYAKOV STUDIO ©SHUTTERSTOCK.COM

BLACK ANGEL BY ROMAN CHAZOV ©SHUTTERSTOCK.COM

PAGE 28:

BABY IMAGE BY ILIYUHA ©123RF.COM

BABY IMAGE 2 BY ROBHAINER ©123RF.COM

BABY IMAGE 3 BY KIWITA ©123RF.COM

PAGE 29:

ILLUSTRATED PEOPLE IMAGE BY LEMBERG VECTOR STUDIO ©SHUTTERSTOCK.COM

PHOTOGRAPHY PEOPLE IMAGES BY RAWPIXEL.COM ©SHUTTERSTOCK.COM

PAGE 30:

MOSAIC OF SAINTS IMAGE BY PETRKURGAN ©123RF.COM

PAGE 31:

MOSAIC OF SAINTS IMAGE BY PETRKURGAN ©123RF.COM

PAGE 32:

MOSAIC OF SAINTS IMAGE BY PETRKURGAN ©123RF.COM

PAGE 33:

ABRAHAM IMAGE BY RUDALL30 ©123RF.COM

MOSES/ARK IMAGE BY RATPACK2 ©SHUTTERSTOCK.COM

PAGE 34:

IMAGES BY RUDALL30 ©123RF.COM

PAGE 35:

IMAGES BY RUDALL30   ©123RF.COM

PAGE 36:
SCRIPT IMAGE BY ANDREYKUZMIN ©123RF.COM

PAGE 39:
SKY IMAGE BY ELENAMIV ©SHUTTERSTOCK.COM
PEOPLE IMAGES BY GRYNOLD ©SHUTTERSTOCK.COM
WAKE ©SHUTTERSTOCK.COM MP2021 ©SHUTTERSTOCK.COM
BENGUHAN ©SHUTTERSTOCK.COM

PAGE 42:
IMAGE BY RUDALL30 © SHUTTERSTOCK.COM

PAGE 44:
WRECK IMAGE BY PHANTOM1311 ©SHUTTERSTOCK.COM

PAGE 45:
PLAGUE IMAGE BY RKATISA ©123RF.COM

PAGE 46:
BRIDGE IMAGE BY AUI MEESRI ©SHUTTERSTOCK.COM
WILDFIRE IMAGE BY BENNY MARTY ©SHUTTERSTOCK.COM
TSUNAMI IMAGE BY RONNIE CHUA ©SHUTTERSTOCK.COM
TSUNAMI IMAGE BY IGORZH ©SHUTTERSTOCK.COM
EARTHQUAKE IMAGE BY DENIS DRYASHKIN ©SHUTTERSTOCK.COM
DROUGHT IMAGE BY DRAGANICA ©SHUTTERSTOCK.COM
HURRICANE BY RYAN DEBERARDINIS ©SHUTTERSTOCK.COM
VOLCANO BY BIERCHEN ©SHUTTERSTOCK.COM

PAGE 47:
ANTI-CHRIST BY WAVEBREAKMEDIAMICRO ©123RF.COM
PRISON PLANET IMAGE BY NOSYREVY ©SHUTTERSTOCK.COM

PAGE 48:
GUILLOTINE IMAGE BY ZEF ART ©SHUTTERSTOCK.COM

PAGE 49:
WAR IMAGE BY IAMSEKI ©SHUTTERSTOCK.COM
PLANET BY PIKE-28 ©SHUTTERSTOCK.COM

PAGE 50:
PLANET BY TOPURIA DESIGN ©SHUTTERSTOCK.COM